GRACE BYERS

I Believe I Can

PICTURES BY **KETURAH A. BOBO**

BALZER + BRAY
An Imprint of HarperCollinsPublishers

Balzer + Bray is an imprint of HarperCollins Publishers.

I Believe I Can

Text copyright © 2020 by Grace Byers

Illustrations copyright © 2020 by Art by Keturah Ariel LLC

All rights reserved. Manufactured in China.

No part of this book may be used or reproduced in any manner whatsoever
without written permission except in the case of brief quotations embodied in
critical articles and reviews. For information address
HarperCollins Children's Books, a division of HarperCollins Publishers,
195 Broadway, New York, NY 10007.
www.harpercollinschildrens.com

Library of Congress Control Number: 2019936751
ISBN 978-0-06-266713-7

Typography by Jenna Stempel-Lobell
19 20 21 22 23   SCP   10 9 8 7 6 5 4 3 2 1
❖
First Edition

To us all:
There will always be one person
who might not believe in you;
let that person never be you. X
—G.B.

To my brothers, Jaryah and Shamir,
and all those who believe in love and optimism
despite the world making you feel as though you cannot
—K.B.

I can sail, like mighty ships.

Like the oceans, I run deep.

I can stretch, just like the Alps,

until I reach my highest peak.

I can charge, just like a train.
Like a rocket, I'll ignite.

Like a star, I can project
my brightest shine against the night.

I am like the lion's roar.

I am like a dragon's flames.

I'm worthy because I'm me,

and there is value to my name.

I can build, just like a brick.

I keep going, like a clock.

I can hold, just like cement.

I can last, just like a rock.

Grounded firm, I'm like the soil.
Like the sky, I'm boundless too.

When I believe in myself,

there's simply nothing I can't do.

Like the hero, I am brave
and face my fears despite my fright.
Because I know I'm not alone,
and in the end, I'll be all right.

Sometimes I am right,
and sometimes I am wrong.

But even when I make mistakes,
I learn from them to make me strong.

I may not win at all I do.
I may experience defeat.

But I'll dust off and try again
to be the best that I can be.

I know my power lies within.

There's nothing that
can hold me down.

There is light within my smile.

There is voice within my sound.

My presence matters in this world.
My life is worthy; there's a plan.

I know I can do anything,

if only
I believe
I can.